Ida's Doll

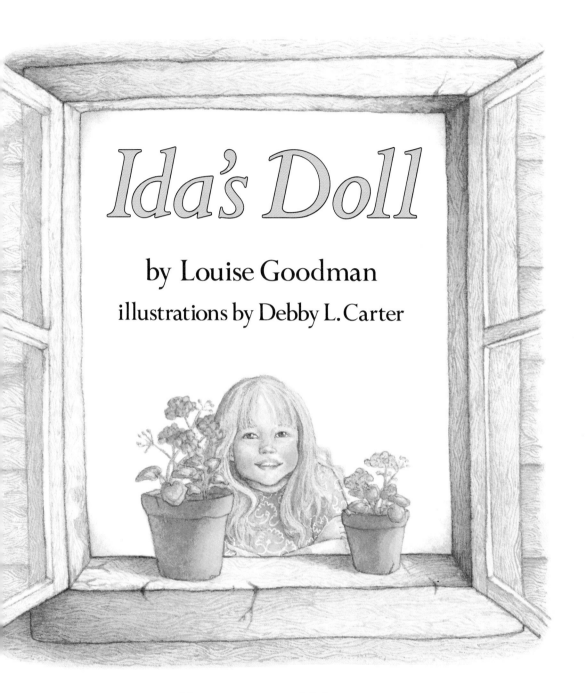

Ida's Doll

by Louise Goodman

illustrations by Debby L. Carter

Harper & Row, Publishers

Library of Congress Cataloging-in-Publication Data

Goodman, Louise.

Ida's doll / by Louise Goodman ; illustrations by Debby L. Carter.—1st ed.

    p.   cm.

  Summary: Bess understands her younger sister's wish for a doll and
does her best to satisfy that wish.

  ISBN 0-06-022275-1 : $

  ISBN 0-06-022276-X (lib. bdg.) : $

  [1. Sisters—Fiction.   2. Dolls—Fiction.]   I. Carter, Debby L., ill.
II. Title.

PZ7.G61378Id   1989   87-25085

[E]—dc19   CIP

                                                    AC

When Ida was a little girl, she lived in
a small village with her grandmother and
her older sister, Bess.

They lived in a small wooden house.
Everything was in one big room. There was a
wooden table where Grandmother kneaded bread,
and the wooden benches where Ida and Bess
sat for all their meals.

In the daytime light streamed through
the windows and made shadows on the floor.

And at night, when the oil lamp was lit,
the big milk pails glowed.

On the cupboard sat Grandmother's silver
candlesticks that Ida loved to polish until
they glistened.

And there was the big black stove. Ida liked
to snuggle under her blanket beside its warmth,
and smell the smells of Grandmother's baking.

During the day Ida played with her friends.
Grandmother called her *little mother duck*
because the other children followed her wherever
she went, like ducklings waddling after their mother.
They would march behind her through the yard

where the chickens clucked and flew around
them like leaves falling from the trees, then
on to the field where the cornstalks hid them,
then to the pond to throw stones that made
ripples on the water and back to the yard again.

On special days Grandmother baked bread
and stuffed a goose. Her cheeks grew rosy as
red apples, and she sang as she worked.

Ida wished she could put her arms around
the sounds and smells and keep them forever.
For her there were never enough times like these—
the wonderful times of being hugged and kissed
and tickled and whooshed through the air.
But they always ended too soon.
The bread had to be taken out of the oven,
the potatoes peeled, the table set
and the oil lamp lit.
If only she had a doll to hug and kiss and tickle.

At night, Ida and Bess climbed the ladder to
the loft where they slept. Their bed was so high,
they had to use a little wooden footstool
to climb into it. Then they would snuggle
under the big quilt filled with goose feathers.
And again, Ida would wish she had a doll to cuddle.
She wished and she wished, though never out loud.

But Bess knew. She remembered
how she had wished for a doll that never came.
And as she watched her little sister,
she wished again. This time
for a doll for Ida.

One night just as they were falling asleep,
Bess had an idea.
She held out her arm for Ida to hold.
Ida smiled, and rocked her sister's arm
and held it close, just as though it were a real doll...
and fell asleep.

From then on, every night she held Bess's arm like a doll. Bess never told Ida how cramped and tired her arm became. How could she, when Ida was sleeping so happily.

One night, as Ida held Bess's arm close, she had a dream.

In her dream the loft had become a
glittering room...and it was *filled* with dolls!
Big dolls and little dolls...fat dolls and skinny dolls...

boy dolls and girl dolls . . . china dolls and straw dolls . . .
dolls whose skin was white or black or yellow or red . . .
dolls that were pretty . . . dolls that were funny. . . .

Ida darted about...
touching and laughing and hugging each doll
until she had played with them all.

She had tea with the china doll...

she danced with the straw doll...

she whooshed the baby doll through the air. . . .

She couldn't decide which one to choose.

The fat doll? The funny doll?

Perhaps the little Indian...
or the funny clown....

Ida sat up.

She looked down at Bess, lying asleep beside her.

Gently, she took Bess's arm...

and held it close and rocked it like a baby...

and with a contented smile,

she drifted off to sleep.